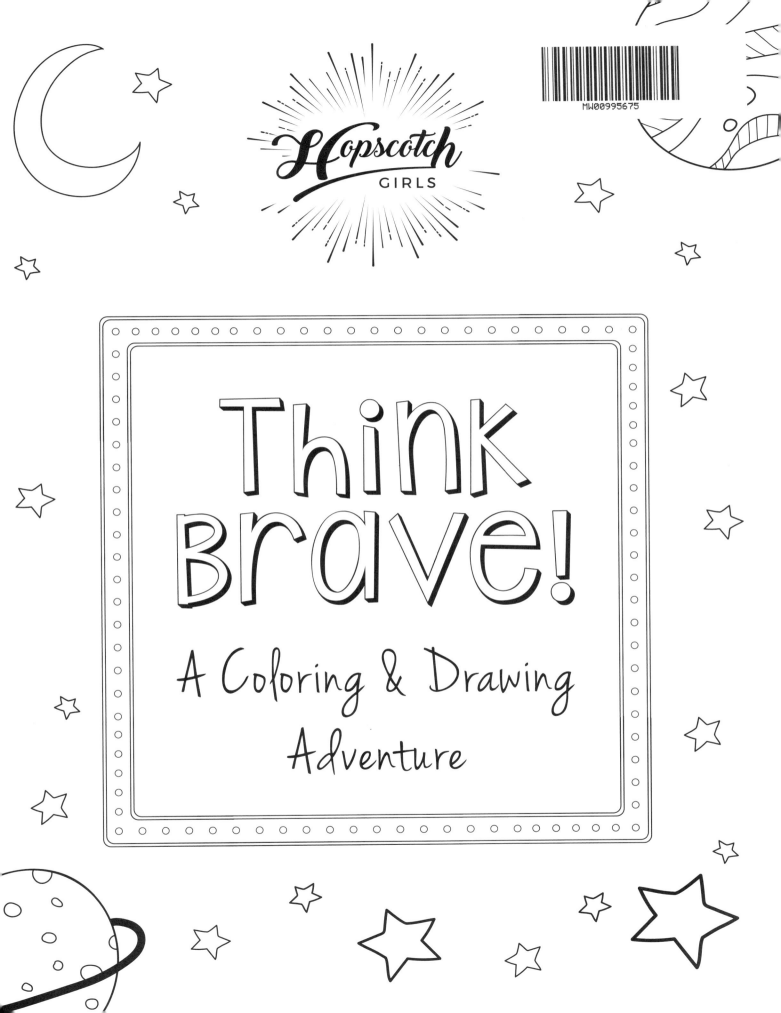

Hopscotch
GIRLS

Think Brave!

A Coloring & Drawing Adventure

Published by Hopscotch Girls
1442 A Walnut St., #131 | Berkeley, CA 94709
ISBN-13: 978-1-7342876-2-2
Printed in the United States
First edition

How to use This Book

Have you ever wondered what it might feel like to drive a train, run for president, or explore a new planet? This is your opportunity to step into an adventure without leaving your home.

This book features 14 exciting adventures for you to enjoy. Each one is an opportunity to get creative—a page for you to color and a page for you to fill in with your own picture.

To get the most out of this book, take a minute to really visualize yourself in each situation before you start drawing. Imagine your surroundings and feelings in that moment. Are you scared? If so, think about how you are going to move beyond that feeling. Are you excited? If so, think about how you'll harness that energy.

You are brave, strong, and determined. You can do it!

For real-life adventures, always be sure to involve a grown-up.

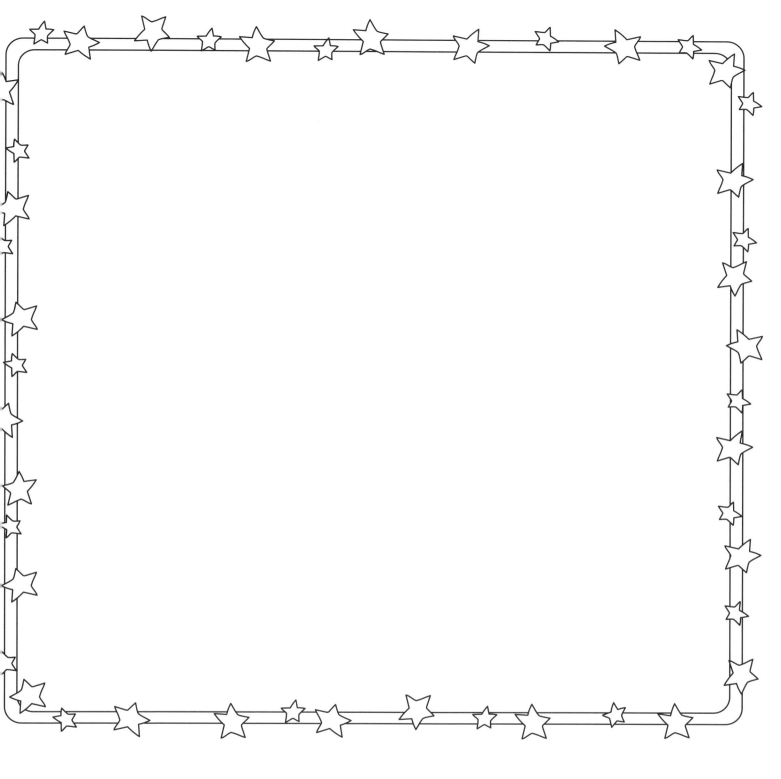

Draw It!

Your spaceship lands with a thud on a new planet. You are the first Earthling there and it's scary, but exciting too. The hatch creaks open and you catch a glimpse of the planet for the first time. Draw yourself exploring this new planet. What do you do? What do you see?

Draw It!

The tallest, twistiest roller coaster in the world is about to take off on its first-ever ride, and you're strapped into the front seat! As the car climbs higher and higher, you look down at the tracks and your heart beats wildly in your chest. Then you feel the car start to speed down the hill as the ride begins. Draw yourself on this thrilling ride.

Draw It!

You speed to a burning home in your fire engine, sirens blaring, dressed in your gear. A family yells and waves to you from a second-story window. They need your help! As flames lap at the house, you jump into action. Draw yourself helping the family and putting out the fire.

Draw It!

You stand on a deserted island with your family. You are stranded with no house, no stores, and no way to get home. It's up to you to help your family find food and make a shelter to sleep in. Draw yourself, your family, and the island home you create.

Draw It!

After hours of hiking, your feet are starting to throb. As the leader of the group, it's your job to guide your friends to the top of the waterfall safely, and you're almost there. You summon your strength and scramble up the last 100 feet, climbing over huge boulders and pulling yourself up over thick roots. Finally, you find yourself at the top of a huge waterfall. Draw yourself at the summit.

Draw It!

You are a trapeze artist, touring with the circus. You stand on a platform, high in the air, your palms sweating as you prepare to begin your flying trapeze act. You look out at the crowd and hear hundreds of people clapping for you. You take a deep breath and leap! Draw yourself swinging from the trapeze.

Draw It!

The crowd cheers wildly around you, waving banners and shouting your name. The match is tied and has gone to penalty kicks. It's up to you to score a goal and win the game for your team. Draw yourself kicking the winning goal.

Draw It!

It's nearly Election Day. You've been campaigning for months with the hope of becoming the next president. You step up to the podium, ready to speak to an audience of thousands about what you believe in and why you should lead the country. Draw yourself speaking to the audience.

Draw It!

Dragons can be extremely dangerous. With one fiery breath, they can turn a house into a pile of ash! No one has ever tamed a dragon before, but you must find a way to make this dragon friendly. The safety of your kingdom depends on you. Draw yourself taming the dragon.

Draw It!

The giant sequoia tree is quite possibly the largest living thing on Earth, and you are about to climb it. Standing at the base of the tree, looking up, the trunk seems to go all the way to the moon! You stretch your hands up, grab on, and begin to climb. Draw yourself climbing the tree.

Draw It!

You pull back the curtains and peek out at the crowd of kids who have gathered for your school talent show. This is your opportunity to show off your true self to the whole school. Your heart pounds as you step out onto the stage. Draw yourself performing for the show. Are you singing? Are you juggling? Think about what you are doing and what makes you special or different.

Draw It!

After studying medicine for years, it's finally time for you to perform your first surgery. You've been preparing for this moment, but you're nervous because you've never done it before. Another doctor nods to you, letting you know it's time to begin. You take a deep breath—you can do this. You are ready to save a life. Draw yourself doing the surgery.

Draw It!

Toot toot! The horn blasts in your ears as you guide the train down the track. As the engineer, you are responsible for getting to the station safely and on time, and you rise to the occasion. Draw the train and yourself driving it.

Draw It!

You look around at your family smiling warmly in the soft light of the restaurant. It's your first night in France, and you're excited to try the local cuisine. A waiter comes to the table and sets a plate in front of you with food you don't recognize. The waiter explains that it's escargot—cooked snails—a delicacy in France. Draw yourself taking a bite.

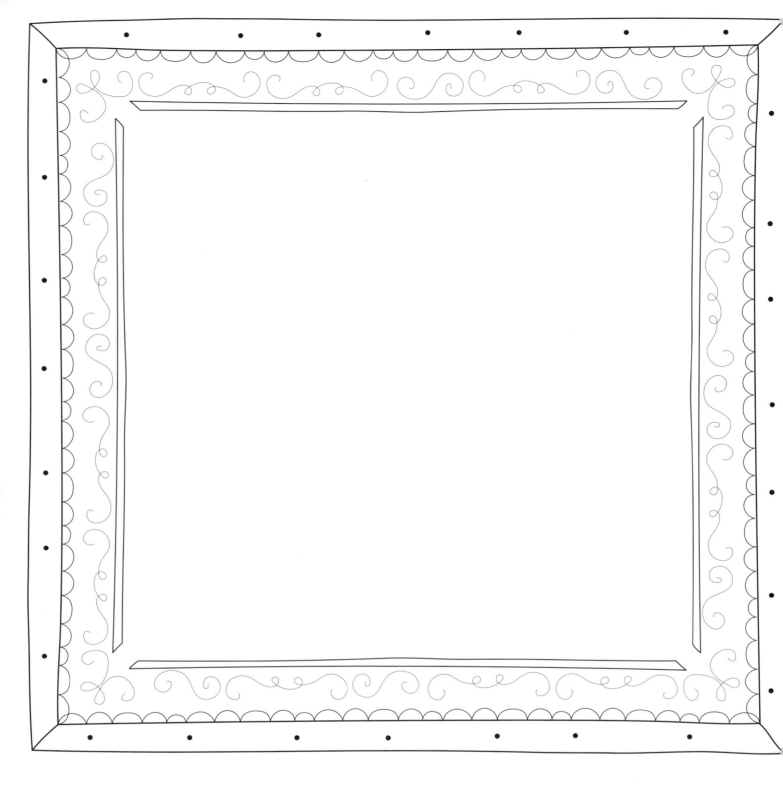

Draw It!

Come up with an adventure of your own and draw it here. Where are you?
What are you doing? How are you feeling?